Be Brave, Morgan!

Morgan on Ice

Morgan

on

by Ted Staunton

illustrated by Bill Slavin

Ice

Formac Publishing Company Limited
Halifax

Formac Publishing Company Limited recognizes the support of the Province of
Nova Scotia through the Department of Communities, Culture and Heritage.
We are pleased to work in partnership with the Province of Nova Scotia
to develop and promote our cultural resources for all Nova Scotians. We
acknowledge the support of the Canada Council for the Arts, which last year
invested $153 million to bring the arts to Canadians throughout the country.
This project has been made possible in part by the Government of Canada.

 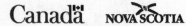

Cover design: Tyler Cleroux
Cover image: Bill Slavin

Library and Archives Canada Cataloguing in Publication

Staunton, Ted, 1956-, author
        Morgan on ice / Ted Staunton ; illustrated by Bill Slavin.

(Be brave, Morgan!)
Reprint. Originally published: Halifax : Formac Publishing
        Company Limited, 2013.
ISBN 978-1-4595-0504-9 (hardcover)

        I. Slavin, Bill, illustrator II. Title. III. Series: Staunton,
Ted, 1956- . Be brave, Morgan!

PS8587.T334M672 2017   jC813'.54   C2017-905333-7

Published by:
Formac Publishing
Company Limited
5502 Atlantic Street
Halifax, Nova Scotia,
Canada, B3H 1G4
www.formac.ca

Distributed in Canada by:
Formac Lorimer Books
5502 Atlantic Street
Halifax, NS, Canada
B3H 1G4

Distributed in the US by:
Lerner Publisher Services
1251 Washington Ave. N.
Minneapolis, MN, USA
55401
www.lernerbooks.com

Printed and bound in Canada.

Manufactured by Friesens Corporation in Altona, Manitoba,
Canada in August 2017.

Job #236683

Contents

Chapter One

Monster Princess

I fall. Aldeen Hummel falls.
Charlie zips by. We get up. I
fall. Tracey swoops past.
Aldeen falls.
Aldeen gets up.
I get up. We both fall.

Matt and Kaely and Mrs.
Ross glide by. "Good for you,
Aldeen! Keep trying, Morgan!"
Mrs. Ross calls.

Our class is skating at the
outdoor rink. We get to skate
once a week.

Everyone
who can skate loves it.
I hate it.

I crawl to the boards and pull myself up. I look back. Aldeen is standing up. Her witchy hair has boinged out from her helmet. Curtis skates by and gives her a push, right at me. "Move!" she yells. I move. I know Aldeen can't turn, and even in a snowsuit, she has knees and elbows like hockey sticks. That's one reason she's the Godzilla of Grade Three.

CLUNK, she hits the boards.
"You should learn how to
stop," I say. Aldeen's eyes

squinch up. Her face is red and her glasses have gone crooked. She pushes at them with her mittens, then wipes where her nose is running at the same time.

At least she can't give noogies with mitts on.

Aldeen has knuckles like hockey sticks too. "You should talk," she says. "Anyway, I'll learn at Princesses On Ice. You

won't. You're not a princess.

So be nice to me or you won't go."

Aldeen was the princess in our class play last term. She still acts like one sometimes. Princesses On Ice is a skating show. Aldeen's Granny Flo won tickets to it from a radio station and asked my mom and me to go with them. Mom says I have to go.

I don't want to go to Princesses On Ice.

I don't like princesses, I don't like ice, and I'm not crazy about Aldeen either.

I haven't told anybody I'm going. Now I keep my mouth shut and inch along the boards. I hate this slidey feeling. I'm supposed to lean forward, like Dad showed me, but all of me is screaming *lean back!* I watch my feet and stretch my arms out. Charlie's voice calls, "Grab my coat." I latch on as he slides by. It will help me stand up. Charlie calls over his shoulder, "Hey Morg,

want to come to Monster-Truck-A-Rama with me?

My dad got tickets."

"Cool," I say. "Thanks! I'll ask my mom and dad." I feel good enough to look up a little. We're picking up speed. I see Charlie holding Tracey holding Chantel holding Will holding Kaely holding Simon holding Matt, which means, oh *no*, it's Crack the Whip!

We're going even faster now, starting to turn. *Uh-oh*, I'm swinging wide. *Double uh-oh*, I can't hold on to Charlie's coat. *Triple uh-oh*, I can't turn either. "*GAAAH*," I sail off like a runaway Zamboni. Dead ahead, wobbling along, with her arms

out and her nose in the air like
a princess, is Aldeen. My own
arms spin like windmills. BAM.
Bring on the monster trucks.

Chapter Two

Man
Up

After school Aldeen comes over to my house. She does that sometimes when her mom and her granny are both working.

"How was skating?" Mom asks. She has hot chocolate for us. Hot chocolate is the only part of skating I like. "It was okay," I say. I know I'm supposed to like skating. Dad plays hockey and Mom used to do figure skating.

"Not as good as Princesses On Ice will be," Aldeen says. She and Mom start talking about it. I don't want to talk about Princesses On Ice. I want to ask Mom if I can go to Monster-Truck-A-Rama.

I'm not going to ask until Aldeen goes, though. She'd probably find a way to wreck everything.

After hot chocolate, Mom
says we need to play outside.
I don't complain. I'm going to
be Super Morgan until I find
out if I can go to Monster
Trucks. Aldeen and I go in the
backyard. My dad has built a
rink there. Aldeen clumps on in
her boots and starts pretending
to be a princess again.

"You get to be my faithful servant," she says.

"No way," I say.

Off comes her mitt.

Up pops her noogie knuckle.

"What do you want?" I ask.

"My royal hockey stick."

I get one. Then I chase the puck every time Aldeen misses the net.

When Aldeen's mom finally picks her up, first thing I do is say to Mom and Dad, "Charlie invited me to Monster-Truck-A-Rama. Can I go? Please?"

"Well, that's nice," Mom says. "I don't see why not. When is it?"

"There's an ad for it right here in the paper," Dad says.

He shows us. There's a picture of an orange monster truck flying over a heap of cars. "Coooool," I say. But Mom says, "Oh, no!

It's the same day as Princesses On Ice."

"Hey," I say, "That means I can't go to Princesses On Ice!" This is great.

"Well, no hon. It means you can't go to Truck-A-Rama.

Aldeen invited you first and you said yes. You can't change your mind. That would be rude."

"But," I say.

"But this is trucks crushing stuff. That's way cooler than —"

"Sorry, Morgan, but that's the way it is."

"Awwwwwwwwwwww."

"Morg," Dad says. "Man up. Thank Charlie, but tell him you

can't go. Then he can invite
someone else. Tell you what,
after dinner why don't we go
out and skate a little?"

I knew Aldeen would find a
way to wreck everything.

Chapter Three

Snow Plan

Next morning I walk to school with Charlie. "I can go," I tell him. I know this is not what I'm supposed to say, but I have a plan. Kind of.

Okay, I don't exactly have a plan, but I'm making one

so I can get out of going to Princesses on Ice and go to Monster-Truck-A-Rama.

I *have* to tell Charlie I can go so he doesn't invite someone else.

All I have to do now is figure out why I can't go to Princesses and Mom still can.

It's tricky.

Since Mom is going, I can't hide and I can't send a blow-up dummy instead of me. She'd be sure to notice.

And if I pretend to be sick or get myself grounded on purpose, I can't go to Truck-A-Rama either.

Charlie and I cross the street with the crossing guard. At the

edge of the school yard, there is a big pile of snow. There's a path around it, but it's way more fun to climb right over it, like mountain climbers. We're almost at the top when I hear a voice from the other side: "You better be nice to me or you're in big trouble. Give it back. Or else."

I know whose voice that is. I peek over the top of the snow bank.

A grade four kid has Aldeen's hat.

It's her favourite one too.

She says it looks like a crown. I remember what Aldeen said to me about being nice, back at the rink, and all at once

I know my plan. If I get Aldeen mad at me, she'll tell me I can't go to Princesses On Ice.

The grade four kid laughs. So do the kids with him. "Or else what?" he says.

Aldeen sweeps out one foot and hooks the kid's ankle. He yells and falls back into the snow bank. Aldeen grabs her hat and shoves a mitt full of snow up his nose before he can do anything.

"Or else that,"

she says. She tugs her hat over her witchy hair and glares at the other kids. Her breath steams like dragon smoke.

They stop laughing.

Aldeen walks away.

On second thought,

maybe getting Aldeen mad

isn't such a great idea after all.

Chapter Four

Potatoes

It takes me till recess to come up with a new plan.

It's a good one.

As we're all putting on our coats and boots, I hear some of the girls talking about figure skating. Aldeen should be friends with them, instead of having to come over to my place all the time.

Then I think, maybe she could be if she invited one of them instead of me. What if she knew one of them wanted to go to Princesses on Ice?

I bet she'd drop me like a hot potato.

All recess long I ask girls about Princesses On Ice. "I think Aldeen has an extra ticket," I say. Two are already going. Three have hockey that day. A bunch say they wouldn't go anywhere with Aldeen. One

says, I'm not allowed to do
stuff with her.

Remember my birthday party when she bit our cat?

Oh yeah.

Finally, just as the bell rings,
Karina says, "She *does*? Wow, I
wish I could go."

"Let's ask her," I say. We get
into line with Aldeen. It's easy
to do: no one lines up too close
to Godzilla. Aldeen looks at us.
At least, I think she does. Her
glasses are kind of foggy above

her scarf. She licks where her nose is running again.

I say, "Karina really wants to go to Princesses On Ice."

Karina says, "Morgan says you might have a ticket."

Aldeen says, "No. I've only got tickets for me and Morgan."

"You're going with *Morgan*?" Karina's eyes get big. "*Ewwwwwww.*" Then she runs off to the other girls. "Hey, guess what? Aldeen's going ..."

Awwwwwww. By the time everybody has coats and boots off, all I can hear is,

"Hey, Prince Charming!"

"No, he's one of the
seven dwarfs!"

"Are you gonna be the frog
again, like in the play?"

"Smoochy-smoochy!"

The whole world knows I'm
going to a princess skating
show with Aldeen Hummel.
That wasn't part of the plan.

Chapter Five

Lies for Lunch

It gets **worse.**

Mrs. Ross gives us math worksheets. My partner is Charlie. He says, "You said you were coming to Truck-A-Rama with me."

"I am," I say. "They're on different days."

"No, they're not. They're both on Saturday."

"I'll take care of it," I tell him.

I don't get much math done. I'm thinking instead about the big lie I'm going to have to tell Aldeen.

At lunch I sit beside her. It's even easier to do than lining up with her. Kids giggle. I pretend not to hear. As soon as Aldeen starts talking about Princesses, I take a deep breath.

"I have to tell you something."

"What?" She crunches a carrot like a T. Rex snapping a leg bone.

I say, "Know how I brought Karina over? And how I'm really bad at skating?"

Aldeen nods. "Not good like me."

Crunch.

"Yeah. That's because I
have, like, this disease where
I'm secretly scared of skating?
I can't even watch it. Ask
my mom. I always run out of
the room when there's figure
skating on TV."

"Right." *Crunch*. "So how come your dad built a rink in your back yard?"

"'Cause he's trying to help me. He keeps saying,

'Man up, Morgan!'

But it doesn't help, it's horrible.

And my mom wants me to go to Princesses On Ice, but I don't know if I can. That's why I thought Karina could go instead of me."

Aldeen doesn't say anything.

I get an idea to make it better. "I mean, what if we go and I go

crazy

and wreck the whole show?"

Aldeen's eyes go squinchy. "You better not. If you do ..." *Crunch.*

I gulp a little. "Hey, just saying." I'm not sure if it's working. I open my lunch and have another idea. "Know what? If you help me, I'll give you my cupcake."

"Is it chocolate?" She grabs the cupcake before I can answer.

"And I get to pick one of your toys too."

Aldeen eats the cupcake.
"I'll call my gran and ask if I
can bring someone else."

Aldeen grabs her stuff and
leaves.

Yesssssss.
I'm a genius.

Mom can still go. I haven't
been rude. I told a lie, but it's a
little one, kind of; a nice lie to
make everyone happy. I'll tell
Karina and Charlie as soon as I
eat my sandwich.

I'm swallowing the last bite
when Aldeen comes back. "I
called from the office. My gran

says I can't invite someone else. It would hurt your feelings."

"WHAT?" I yell. "What did you tell her?"

"What I said. I asked could I bring someone else."

"BUT —"

"Man up," says Aldeen, "and you owe me a toy."

Chapter Six

Men
Up

After school Aldeen comes
over again. She and Mom talk
about how cool Princesses will
be again. At least she doesn't
blab on me. Instead, she takes
my Commander Crunch 4X4
Remote Control Zoom Buggy

that will drive over almost
anything. "Awwwwww," I say.

"Man up,"
she says.

Dad gets home just after
Aldeen goes. The phone rings
while he's making a yucky
salad and Mom and I are setting
the table. Dad answers.

"Hello? Oh, hi, how are you?"
He jokes around for a little,

then listens and says, "Really? I don't — hang on, I'll check." He looks mixed up. Dad covers the phone and says, "It's Bill, Charlie's dad. He wants to know if Morgan is going to Truck-A-Rama with them on Saturday."

Now Mom looks mixed up. "Well no, we're going to Princesses On Ice with Aldeen and Flo. I thought they knew that."

"Me too," Dad nods. He says into the phone, "Doesn't look like it, Bill. Morgan must have mixed the date up. Thanks, though."

Dad hangs up. He and Mom look at me.

I shrug and have to tell another little kind-of lie.

It's only kind of because it's partly mostly true. "I dunno. I told him I really wanted to go." Then I try to look kind of sad, like a kid who never gets anything special.

Maybe it works, because Mom says, "I know, hon. But we'll have fun too."

Then she hands me the forks. I guess it didn't work that well.

"Oh, I'm sure you will," Dad says. Mom shoots him a look.

It's time for dessert, my favourite part of dinner,

when the phone rings again.
Mom answers this time. When
she hangs up, she sighs, "Bad
news. Grandma's away this
weekend and Grandpa needs
me to help get him to his
doctor's appointment. I can't go
to Princesses On Ice."

Oh *yesssssssss*. This is better than dessert.

If Mom can't go ... I jump up. "I better call Charlie," I say.

"Whoah" says Mom, "Hold your horses, mister. Just because I can't go doesn't mean you can't. Dad will go with you instead."

"What?" Dad says, "But —"

"Man up," Mom says.

Chapter Seven

Bulldozer Blades

It gets worse. When I get to school the next morning, I find out Charlie has asked Will to go to Monster-Truck-A-Rama instead.

Now I'm sunk.

The rest of the day, all I hear
are Prince Charming jokes and
Aldeen saying things like, "I
wonder how Sleeping Beauty
will skate?" When I say "Really
slowly," she noogies me.

After school, Charlie comes back to my place too. He brings his skates. Aldeen left hers at my place already. After snacks we go out back to Dad's rink.

Boy, do I ever wish spring would come.

Aldeen starts scraping
across the ice. She has her
crown hat on again. "I'm a
princess," she says. Charlie
skates around her like a
superstar. He can even go
backwards.

I start at one end but I can't

turn. I flop into the piled-up snow at the other. I make a pretty big dent.

"I'm a monster truck on skates,"

I tell Charlie.

"That's because you don't know how to turn," he says. "Look, I'll show you."

He shows me how he crosses one foot over the other. "Try it," he says.

I try it, but as I cross over, I hear "Look out, bozo!" I look up and Aldeen is coming right at me with her hands stuck out, like a bulldozer on blades. WHAM! We both go down.

"Monster truck crash,"

Charlie cheers. "I hope they do that on Saturday."

"Where?" says Aldeen, sitting up and pushing her glasses back.

"At Monster-Truck-A-Rama," Charlie says. "On Saturday. I'm going with Will." He looks at me. I'm flat on my back. I don't feel like a monster truck anymore.

I feel like a marshmallow.

I get up. Charlie shows us both how to cross our feet over when we turn. We try it. I'm shakey but I start to get it; I really start to get it. So does Aldeen; she gets it quicker than me, even. Pretty soon she's zooming past me. It's harder to turn one way than the other though, and there's still one little problem: neither of us knows how to stop. WHAM. We both hit the ice again.

"Can't you learn how to stop?" I complain.

"I don't have to," Aldeen says. "I'm a monster truck."

Chapter Eight

Super Sulk

By the time Aldeen and Charlie leave, **I've had enough of skating, princesses, monster trucks, winter, everything.**

And I want my Commander Crunch Zoom Buggy too.

I guess it doesn't matter
what I want, because
everything just gets worse. It's
Dad's night to make dinner and
he makes vegetable stir fry.

I hate vegetable
stir fry.

I can't even hide the vegetables under the noodles, because the noodles are the only part I eat.

The only good thing is that Mom doesn't bug me too much about not eating because she doesn't like vegetable stir fry either.

I think that bugs Dad, so by the time we all flop on the couch to watch TV after dinner, we're all **grumpy**.

And then the very first thing that comes on is an ad for Princesses On Ice. It's all princes and princesses swooning around on skates and gliding into each other's arms. Dad and I look at each other. "Oh, *yuck*," I whisper. "I'll second that," Dad murmurs.

Mom folds her arms. "Hey, you two. This is something that means a lot to Aldeen, and she wants to share it with you. Keep behaving that way and all you'll do is spoil it for everyone."

Dad sighs and sits up. "Okay. Mom's right, Morg. It was nice of Aldeen to invite us. We can still have fun if we want to, right? We're in this together. We can all get pizza after."

"I guess," I say.

Pizza makes just about anything better.

But it still feels as if I don't have much choice. I think that if Aldeen really wanted to be nice, she could have invited someone else.

"And you know what?" Dad says, jumping up. "Instead of sitting here sulking, let's all do something fun right now. Let's all put our skates on and hit the rink. Mom can show us some figure skating moves and you can show us how you learned to turn, from Charlie."

"Perfect," says Mom. She
jumps up too and zaps off the
TV with the remote.

I don't even bother to say
"Awwwwwwww."

Chapter Nine

Skate Exchange

Aldeen and her Granny Flo pick us up on Saturday afternoon. Granny Flo is wearing her leather taxi driver jacket. She's smoking one of her little cigars out the window as they wait for us to climb in.

As we pull away, Granny

Flo says, "Change of plans, boys. Hope you don't mind. The radio station I won the tickets from let me swap them for the other prize. We've got tickets for Monster-Truck-A-Rama instead."

"Truck-A-Rama!"
I blast up in my seat.

"Yeah," Granny Flo chuckles. "Should have known Aldy would want to go, but she'd been talking so much about princesses that I never thought about it. Then she came home yesterday yakking up a storm about it."

I look at Aldeen. "I thought you liked princesses too," I say.

"Not as much as monster trucks.

Crunching is more fun than princessing.

Everybody knows that."

I try to decide which hurts
less:

getting crunched by Monster Truck Aldeen or noogied by Aldeen the Princess.

Right now it doesn't matter.
This feels good.

We drive to the domed
stadium. It's huge. Our seats
are way up near the roof. I
look all over to see if I can
spot Charlie and Will. I can't.
Some of the seats are so far
away, the people in them are

just little dots. "I shoulda brought my binoculars," says Granny Flo.

Maybe it's because we're so far away, but, Monster-Truck-A-Rama is, well, boring. It's long, loud, and stinky. Even the hot dogs are yucky. From our seats the trucks look like toys, and a lot of the time there's so much dust that you hardly see them. You can't tell how good the crunches are. I wonder if Charlie and Will can see them.

After a while the most interesting thing to watch is an ad on the Jumbo Screen. It's for a new 3D movie called

Elfquest. It's coming soon and it looks really cool, even if there is a princess, because there are dragons too, and sword fights. The ad plays a bunch of times between ads for cars and boring stuff. When I see Aldeen watching it too, I say, "Cool, huh?"

"Yeah," she says, "but the dragon doesn't look very scary." She's right.

Aldeen looks scarier herself sometimes.

I don't say that though. Instead, Aldeen says, "Can we go soon?"

"You want to go before it's over?" Granny Flo raises her eyebrows. We nod.

Dad says, "What would you two like to do instead?"

Before I can say anything, Aldeen says, "Skate."

I look at her. What really surprises me is that I say,

"Me too."

Chapter Ten

Go with the Flo

"Sounds good to me," says Granny Flo. "Let's go," says Dad.

On the way out, we see Charlie and Will and Charlie's dad. **"It was boring,"** they say.

"Want to come back to our place and skate?" I ask.

"Sure!"

So everybody comes over. It's the most people ever on our rink. I cross my feet over a couple of times when I'm turning. Mom starts teaching me how to stop.

I think I'm starting to get it.

I don't fall down as much, anyway.

We even have a little hockey game. Granny Flo plays goal; she's good too, especially with her glove. "Used to play in a league," she says.

"Really?" Aldeen snorks. Her nose is running again.

"Sure. 'Go with the Flo' they used to say."

"Cool," everyone says. A few minutes later, Aldeen crashes into me. This time she's not a princess or a monster truck.

"I'm a hockey player,"

she says.

I'm extra hungry by the time we go in for pizza. Mom reminds me to be polite and share. "And don't forget to thank Aldeen's granny for taking you," she says.

I'm so polite I don't even take the last piece of pizza, even though it's sitting there all by itself. I haven't said thanks yet though. Dad gives me a nudge. I say, "Thank you for taking me," to Aldeen and her Granny Flo.

"No problem," says Aldeen. "You can take me to *Elfquest*."

Then she takes the last piece of pizza.

More titles in **Be Brave, Morgan!**

Morgan the Brave

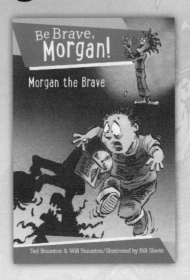

Morgan has to figure out how to go to a birthday party— but avoid seeing the scary movie promised as the main event. Birthday boy Curtis tries to expose anyone missing out on his party as a chicken, so Morgan needs an idea, and quick! Is it possible that Aldeen, Morgan's frenemy who never fails to notice and taunt him about his weaknesses, has the solution? Morgan finds that not everyone is as tough as they look.

Daredevil Morgan

Be Brave, **Morgan!**

Daredevil Morgan

Ted Staunton/Illustrated by Bill Slavin

Morgan's best friend Charlie urges him to try the GraviTwirl ride at the Fall Fair. But Morgan is focused on his homegrown contender for the Perfect Pumpkin contest. That is, until Aldeen Hummel, the Godzilla of Grade Three, drops it!

Morgan faces Aldeen in a bumper car War. Aldeen dares him to go on the Asteroid Belt ride. Will Morgan be brave enough to try? And can he still win the Best Pumpkin Pie contest with the remains of his squished squash?

Morgan's Got Game

Be Brave, **Morgan!**

Morgan's Got Game

50

Ted Staunton/Illustrated by Bill Slavin

Morgan is left out of the loop when everyone at school begins bringing their Robogamer Z7 to school, linking up online with one another, and playing at recess and lunch. Charlie lets Morgan use his Z7 every now and then, but clearly you're not cool unless you have one of your own.

Poor Morgan is reduced to playing other games with Aldeen for something to do. Finally his parents relent, but Morgan learns that sometimes gaming is more trouble than it's worth!